Pitt Street Pirates

by

Terry Deary

Illustrated by

You do not need to read this page - just get on with the book!

Published in 2004 in Great Britain by
Barrington Stoke Ltd, Sandeman House, Trunk's Close,
55 High Street, Edinburgh EH1 1SR

This edition based on *Pitt Street Pirates*, published by
Barrington Stoke in 2001

ISBN 1-84299-208-2

Printed in Great Britain by Bell & Bain Ltd

Meet The Author – Terry Deary

What is your favourite animal?
A rat
What is your favourite boy's name?
Marmaduke
What is your favourite girl's name?
Bertha
What is your favourite food?
Horse
What is your favourite music?
Bagpipes
What is your favourite hobby?
Singing to bagpipes

Meet The Illustrator – Steve Donald

What is your favourite animal?
A goldfish
What is your favourite boy's name?
Kieran
What is your favourite girl's name?
Elizabeth
What is your favourite food?
Scrambled eggs
What is your favourite music?
1970s' pop music
What is your favourite hobby?
Playing on the computer

To Kath, with love

SD

Contents

Before We Start ...
Meet the Pitt Street Pirates!

ROGER REDBEARD

Captain of the Pitt Street Pirates, and master of crime. He calls himself Redbeard but doesn't have a beard! In fact, he's too young to shave – and he *never* washes behind his ears.

Pitt Street Pirates

ELLIE FLYNN

Not as big as a gorilla and not as pretty – but a lot stronger. Only two weak spots – chocolate and Roger Redbeard.

SNIFFLE SMITH

Weak and weedy member of the gang, he has all the brains of a tin can – an empty tin can. So why is he there at all?

Pitt Street Pirates

MINNIE

Ship's parrot. The only four-legged parrot in the whole of Pitt Street.

Chapter 1
A Pitt Street Plan

Roger Redbeard didn't have a red beard.

"Why are you called Redbeard then?" Sniffle Smith, his weedy friend, asked.

"Because *all* my family are called Redbeard," Roger told him. "Why are you called Sniffle?"

"Dunno," Sniffle sniffed. "*Sn-Sn-Sn-iff*! Was your dad called Redbeard?"

5

Roger put a hand on his thick, *black* hair. "I never met my dad," he said.

"So, does your *mum* have a red beard?" Sniffle asked.

Roger gave a sigh. Sniffle was as thick as they come. "The Redbeards took their name from Captain Redbeard. He was a great pirate!" Roger said with pride.

"What sort of planes did he fly?" Sniffle asked.

"P-I-R-A-T-E. Pirate, you dummy! Not *pilot!*" Roger said. "The terror of the high seas. Robber of Spanish gold."

Sniffle gave a sigh. "I wish we were pirates. I'd like to find some gold."

Roger looked hard at the shabby houses across the street. He closed his eyes ... and saw them in his mind as great ships.

Galleons under full sail. "Why not, Sniffle? Why not?"

"Er ... is it that we haven't got a ship?" Sniffle asked.

"We'll build one! Mr Clark at the corner shop has stacks of old wooden boxes! We'll build a ship and sail the seven seas."

"But I have to be back in time for supper," Sniffle said.

"Then we'll sail the seven park lakes!" Roger shouted and jumped to his feet. He ran down the street to the corner shop. Sniffle walked slowly after him. Out of some dark corner came a cat. A skinny, flea-bitten cat with one ear missing. They called her Minnie.

****

Roger Redbeard was the first of his family for 400 years to build a pirate ship. And the first one *ever* to build it in his back yard. Sniffle sniffed when he saw it.

"It'll never float!"

"Hah! That's what they said about the *Titanic*!" Roger said, with a grin.

"Did they?" asked Sniffle.

"They did! And look where the *Titanic* ended up!" he said.

"I see!" Sniffle smiled – but he didn't see. He still felt unhappy. "Can I be Captain?" he asked.

"You can be Cabin Boy," Roger told him. "You can go up into the crow's nest up top and keep a look out."

"Is that a big job?"

"You can't get any higher," Roger grinned.

After hours of hard work the boat was ready. There were just one or two problems.

"How do we get it down to the lake?" asked Sniffle.

"What a stupid thing to ask," Roger replied. "How do they get a ship in a bottle?"

"I don't know," said Sniffle.

"Well, there you are!" Roger cried.

"But it won't go through the gate!" Sniffle said.

"It came in, didn't it?" Roger grinned again.

But Sniffle was right.

"Push!" the Captain told him. Sniffle pushed. The boat didn't move. "You push and I'll pull!" Roger told him.

The Cabin Boy pushed one end and the Captain pulled the same end. The boat didn't move. Captain Redbeard stroked his chin – with no red beard on it. "We need more help," he said. "And I know just where to get it!"

Roger set off up the steps and along the passage to Flat 13.

Chapter 2
A Mighty Mate

In Flat 13, Ellie was lying on her bed. It was a huge bed. Ellie was a big girl. She was reading a book and watching an old black-and-white film. She was clever like that – she could do two things at once.

Sniffle could never do two things at once.

Ellie heard the rap at the door. "Come in!" she called.

Roger kicked the door open. *Crack.*

"Roger!" Ellie cried and gave him a hug. "You don't know how long I've waited for this moment," she sighed.

"What moment?" Roger blinked.

"Why, the moment when you walked in here just to see me. What do you want, darling?" she asked gently.

"He wants some fish," Sniffle said.

"I'm Captain Roger Redbeard. And I need help to get my new ship into the water," he told her.

Ellie jumped off the bed. "Oh, are you playing at pirates? Can I join the crew?"

"Not *playing*," Roger said. "And you don't get women pirates."

"Yes, you do. There's one in the opera, *The Pirates of Penzance*. She's called Ruth," Ellie said at once.

"Well," Roger said, "my crew of pirates are going to be Ruth-*less*. Hee! Hee! Hee! Get it? *Ruth*-less!"

Sniffle smiled. But he didn't see the joke.

"OK, but then you don't get the boat in the water," said Ellie with a shrug.

"You're in the crew," Roger said at once. "First Mate."

"She could have my job in the cow's nest," Sniffle offered.

"Crow's nest," Roger hissed.

"Just as you say."

"No. She wouldn't fit."

Ellie led the way to the door. "*Avast and belay there!*" she cried. (She'd read the right pirate books.)

"Er, how do I do that?" Sniffle asked.

Roger gave a shrug and went into the yard with Ellie.

Ellie looked at the ship. "It'll never float," she said sadly.

Sniffle smiled. What had Roger told him? "That's what they said about the *Titanic*! And look where it ended up!"

"At the bottom of the sea," said Ellie. "It hit an iceberg."

There was no reply to that. Sniffle sniffled. *Sn-Sn-Sn-iff*!

Roger looked at her. He was cross. "Are you going to say it won't go through the gate?" he snapped.

"Yeah," the Cabin Boy cut in. "Well, how do they get bottles in ships? Eh?"

Ellie smiled. "Never mind. It can go *over* the wall." And she picked up the galleon and carried it towards the street. Roger put a hand under the ship. "OK, Ellie, I've got it!"

Ellie lifted the ship onto the top of the wall and ran through the gate to catch it as it slid into the back lane. Then she marched off towards Pitt Street Park. The Captain, the Cabin Boy and the skinny cat went running after her.

Small kids rushed to their doors to look at the splendid sight. A galleon in full sail down Pitt Street!

"What are you going to call her, Roger?" Mr Clark called out as the ship passed the corner shop.

Roger had a quick think. "Er ... the *Titanic*!" he called.

Old Mr Clark shook his head. "Hope there are no icebergs down on the park pond."

There were no icebergs. But there were lots of kids with sailboats and motorboats of all shapes and sizes.

When the Pitt Street Pirates and the *Titanic* got to the edge of the lake, the kids ran away to hide in the bushes as if they'd seen a mad dog. Soon the pond was empty.

Ellie slid the ship onto the grass at the edge of the lake.

"How's that, Captain?" she asked.

Roger gave a shrug. "Not bad. But you didn't have to carry it *all* the way. Sniffle and I could have done it on our own, you know."

"Aye, aye, Captain," Ellie said in a humble voice.

Roger Redbeard patted his good ship with pride. "I name this ship *Titanic*. Er ..."

"May God bless her and all who sail in her," Ellie added.

"I was *just* going to say that," Roger snapped. "May dogs get her and all who fail in her!" He gave the ship a great push to send her sliding into the cruel sea.

Sniffle cheered.

Minnie the cat purred.

Ellie clapped.

But the *Titanic* didn't budge. She had made up her mind to stay on the shore.

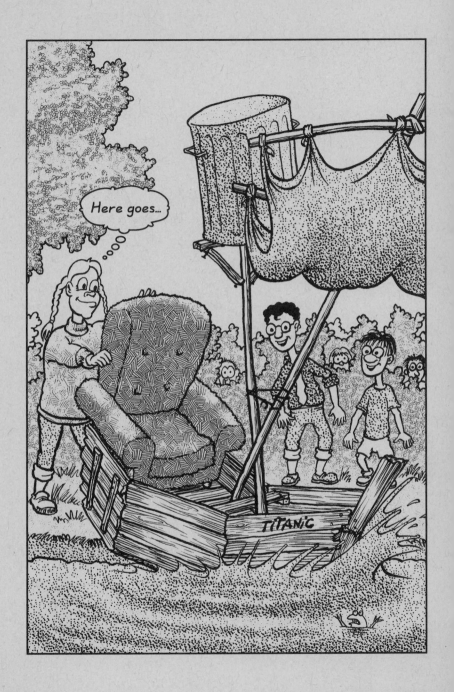

Chapter 3
A Treasure Island

Fifty kids were watching from the bushes in Pitt Street Park as Ellie stepped up to the galleon and pushed her gently towards the water. Fifty kids were silent as the *Titanic* hit the water with a splash. Fifty kids and Ellie and a cat gasped as the ship bobbed happily up and down on the water.

"It floats!" Ellie said.

Roger gave a shrug and tried not to look too pleased. "What did you think it would do?" he asked.

"Float, Captain," said Ellie and grinned. "Shiver me timbers."

"Er ... shiver your what?" asked Roger.

"Me timbers, Captain. That's what all the pirates say," Ellie told him.

"Do they?" Roger blinked. "You seem to know a lot about it."

"I've read all the books, seen all the films. I know all about pirates!" she told him.

"Uh-huh? Anything else you think I should know about them?"

"Don't worry. I'll tell you all at the pirates' den tonight."

"Pirates' *den*?" Sniffle cut in.

"That's right. My room," Ellie went on happily. "Ship's biscuits and grog!"

"I don't like frogs," Sniffle said.

Roger just shook his head. This pirate stuff was a lot harder than he'd thought. "All aboard the *Titanic*!" he cried, and he stepped off the bank onto the swaying ship.

Sniffle followed. He had a hard time getting up to the crow's nest at the top of the mast. The mast was weak and it swayed a bit.

The ship sank a little lower in the water as Ellie joined them with a cry of, "Shiver me timbers!"

Minnie the cat jumped on board just as Ellie pushed them off from the shore with a bit of wood. She used it to paddle them out

into the lake. Roger grabbed the rudder and tried to steer.

Roger closed his eyes. Now he could see the seven seas ahead of them. "Tiver me shimbers!" he yelled. He looked up to the top of the mast. "Can you see anything, Mr Cabin Boy?" he cried.

Sniffle pointed back to the shore. "A Spanish galleon, Captain!" he called back.

Roger swung round. There, on the shore, was a little girl. She stood and glared at them. She had the most white and frilly dress Roger had ever seen.

"I say! You people in that boat! Come here at once!" she ordered.

"Turn the ship around and go back, Ellie!" Roger said.

"You mean *avast and belay*, don't you?" the First Mate asked.

"Do I?" replied the dazed Captain.

"Aye, aye, Sir!" Ellie cried and paddled back to the shore.

Roger stared at the girl who stood there. She had small blue bows in her hair. But he wasn't looking at her hair. He was looking at her cycle. It was a three-wheeler and it glittered like a galleon full of gold.

The *Titanic* bumped up against the shore and Sniffle fell into the lake. "Help! Roger! Help! I can't swim. Help! I'm drowning!" he wailed.

"No, you're not," Ellie said, with a sigh. "The water's only up to your knees. Stand up, Cabin Boy."

Sniffle gave a silly grin and dripped his way out of the lake.

"Now," the girl on the golden cycle said, "I want you to take me out to the island in the middle of the lake on your boat."

Roger just gazed at her and Sniffle just grinned. Ellie looked angry. "Why should we?"

The little girl tossed her curls and said, "Because I'm Ruby Rose."

"I'm sorry to hear that," Sniffle said.

"My daddy is the mayor of this town, Mayor Rupert Rose," Ruby went on. "The town golf club is having a Fun Day for children. It's my job to sort out the treasure hunt."

"Treasure!" said Roger, excited.

"I plan to hide a clue on that island in the lake," Ruby told them. "So take me across in that raft of yours."

"Yes, Miss," Roger said.

"No way," Ellie snapped.

"Wait a moment," said Roger to Ellie. "I *am* the Captain."

"Sorry, Sir," Ellie said in a low voice. "But we can make some money out of this. She'll have to pay us!"

Roger looked excited. "Yeah!" he said to Ruby. "It'll cost you ten pence ..."

"A pound!" Ellie said.

"OK!" Ruby Rose agreed. "I'll pay you when we're safely back."

And they set off across the lake again with Miss Ruby Rose aboard.

The Pitt Street Pirates sailed in silence. They had to, Ruby talked so much. "This will be the last clue but one. If they solve this one, they'll find the one that tells them where the treasure is," she told them. She pulled a slip of paper from her frilly, white bag and held it under Roger's nose. It said ...

In Pitt Street Park, up a tree somewhere within THIS LAND I'll be.

"Get it?" Ruby said with a grin.

Roger shook his head. "Good!" said Ruby. "Only the really brainy ones will get the answer."

"Can I look?" Ellie asked. Ellie looked at the paper. "Easy," she said.

Ruby's face turned an angry red. "No, it's not! There are hundreds of trees in Pitt Street Park."

"But only one on the island," Ellie said softly.

"How do you know it's on the island?" asked Ruby crossly.

"The clue says, 'Somewhere within THIS LAND'." Ellie had worked it out. "Take the I-S from THIS and the L-A-N-D and you have I-S-L-A-N-D. Island!"

"Land ahoy!" Sniffle cried.

"Hah!" Ruby said with a nasty grin. "You only knew that because that's where we're going."

"Land a-hoyyyy!" Sniffle yelled.

"Oh no, I didn't!" Ellie told her sharply.

"Oh yes, you did!"

"Land a-HOYYYY!!" yelled Sniffle again.

"Oh no, I didn't!"

"Oh yes, you ... eeeeek!"

Ccccrrrunnnch! The *Titanic* hit the island.

"Land a-h-e-e-e-lp!" Sniffle cried as he sailed from the crow's nest and landed at the top of the island's only tree.

"Abandon ship!" Roger cried as he climbed ashore.

"My daddy will have you punished!" Ruby cried, as green water lapped over her shiny red shoes.

"Sorry, Captain," Ellie said with a sheepish smile as the *Titanic* sank in the shallow water.

Chapter 4

A Four-Legged Parrot

Ellie lifted Sniffle down from the tree. Then Ruby gave her the treasure hunt clue. "Put that up in the tree!" she ordered.

This time Ellie didn't argue with her. She put her large hand as high up in the tree as she could reach.

Sniffle was taking bits of twig out of his nose. "How do we get back, Captain Roger?" he asked.

Roger was looking sadly at the huge hole in the *Titanic's* side. "Swim," he said.

"I can't swim!" Sniffle told him.

"And I *won't*!" Ruby said and stamped her slimy sock. "I'll just wait here till Daddy's helicopter comes to fetch me ... but you'll have to pay for the fuel," she warned.

"I guess I'll have to carry you back," Ellie said. "The water's not too deep for me."

So Ellie carried Ruby over to the shore and Roger carried Sniffle. Minnie sat on Sniffle's head.

"Mind you don't splash that smelly water on my best dress!" Ruby said. "Cost a thousand pounds in Paris, this did! And I

don't think much of *your* dress, my dear Ellie! It's only fit to clean the floor with."

When Ellie got to the shore Ruby ordered, "Put me down."

Ellie turned and walked back to the edge of the lake. She put Ruby down. She put her down in the deepest, most weedy part of the lake she could find.

Ruby came up spitting out tadpoles. "You'll be hearing from my daddy!" Ruby yelled as the Pitt Street Pirates ran off into the narrow, dusty streets. They would be safe there. They could hear Ruby wailing as she dripped towards her cycle. "Oh, no! Someone's stolen my hubcaps!"

Roger panted as they ran, "We didn't get that pound off her."

Ellie grinned. "Never mind. I've got something much better!" She opened her fist and waved a slip of paper under Roger's nose. "I've got the last clue to the treasure hunt. Solve the clue and get the prize! Meet me tonight in the pirates' den!"

****

Later that evening, Ellie switched off her TV and smiled. "That pirate in the film was doing just what pirates have to do!" she said.

"Just like my Auntie Jane," Sniffle said.

"Is your Auntie Jane a pirate?"

"No, but she does what she has to do."

"Shut up, Sniffle," said Roger with a sigh.

"Yes, Captain Roger."

"And what was that song again ... *me hearty?*" Captain Redbeard asked his Mate.

"*Fifteen men on the dead man's chest, Yo-ho-ho and a bottle of rum,*" Ellie said.

Sniffle shook his head. "That song's no good for me, Captain."

"Why not?" asked Roger.

"I can't count up to 15. I only have 10 fingers."

"You stupid land blubber ..." Roger snarled.

"*Lubber!*" Ellie said. "*Land lubber.*"

"Yeah!" Roger nodded. "He's one of those, too. I'll have you talking to tanks!"

"*Walking the plank*," Ellie said gently.

"Yeah, that's it! Walking the plank!" Captain Redbeard turned to Ellie. "Am I starting to sound like a real pirate?" he asked.

"Oh, much better," she smiled. "And of course you're *much* better looking!"

"Of course," Roger agreed.

"Now all we need are the clothes," she went on. "I've made scarves for Sniffle and me."

Sniffle sniffed with joy as he saw the bright red silk scarves. "Where did you get the silk?" he gasped.

"Mum's knickers," she said.

"Won't she miss them?"

"Not until it gets a bit colder," said Ellie.

"I'm not having knickers on my head," Roger said.

"Oh, no," Ellie told him sweetly. "I made *this* for you." And she pulled out a black pirate hat that just fitted Roger's head. "Now you're a real pirate captain," she said.

"Yeah!" Captain Redbeard said, as he looked at himself with pride in the cracked mirror.

He undid his shirt to the waist, kicked off his shoes and strutted up and down the room. "Are we all ready to go now?"

Ellie shook her head. "You need a parrot."

"Where will we get a parrot in Pitt Street?" Sniffle asked.

Ellie looked at Minnie the cat. All at once, her long arm shot out and she grabbed the cat. With her other hand, she tied a bit of elastic round Minnie's head and clamped a beak made of card onto her nose. She put the puzzled cat on Roger's shoulder. "*Now* we are a pirate crew!" she said.

"Without a ship," Sniffle pointed out.

"Ah, but with a treasure chest to find," she said. "Let's work out this last clue to Ruby Rose's treasure hunt. We'll be able to buy a hundred ships by this time tomorrow," she told them.

The treasure is there
if you seek deep down
in the jumbled EARTH
of the MATCHES BROWN

Chapter 5
The Crooked Cow

"I'll read the clue," Ellie said. She unfolded the grubby slip of paper which Ruby had given her to put up in the tree.

"That's it!" Roger cried. "It says 'matches brown' ... the matches you can buy in Brown's shop, do you think?"

"I don't think so," Ellie told him.

But Roger just went on talking. "Do you know any shops owned by a Mr or Mrs Brown?" he asked Sniffle.

Sniffle blinked. "Old Bully Brown runs the *Crooked Cow* pub in Dock Street."

Roger punched the air, "That's it!" Then he punched his Cabin Boy on the arm. "Well done, Sniffle! Well done! Maybe you're not as stupid as you look."

Roger jumped to his feet. "We just have to dig in the earth in the back yard of the *Crooked Cow*!"

"No!" Ellie said. "You don't understand ..."

"Hey!" Sniffle looked scared. "That's a pretty tough place! They say that Baby-face Ging's gang used to hang out there in the old days. It was their hide-out."

Roger was making for the door with the cat on his shoulder. Ellie grabbed Sniffle's hand and ran after him. "Why would Ruby Rose want to hide treasure down in that part of town?" she argued.

Roger grabbed a garden trowel from a window box as he rushed out into the cool night air. "The clue is in the word *jumbled*, Roger!" the girl tried to tell him. "It means the letters are all mixed up to make another word."

But Roger didn't hear her. He sailed on down the dark street with Ellie and Sniffle trailing behind him.

"You see," Ellie was saying, "mix up the letters in BROWN MATCHES to make new words and you get TOWN CHAMBERS. That's where the Town Council meets. That's where a girl like Ruby Rose would

hide the treasure. You understand, Sniffle,
don't you?"

"Er ... no, Ellie."

But Ellie went on. "The letters E-A-R-T-H
can be changed to make HEART. And the
letters in B-R-O-W-N M-A-T-C-H-E-S make
TOWN CHAMBERS. See?"

"Er ... no, Ellie."

"The treasure's in the Town Chambers!"
she told them.

Sniffle shook his head. "Captain Roger
was right about the *Titanic*," he told her.
"He'll be right this time, too."

"Yes," she said. "He's a great Captain
and a fantastic ship-builder ... but he's no
good at word games!"

Still Roger rushed on down the dark streets muttering, "*Avast and belay there, me hearties. Pieces of eight and Spanish gold!*" The tooting of the tug boats broke the silence of the dark streets as they came near the old dock area of the town.

The damp river air made Ellie shiver.

The shapes in the shadows made Sniffle shake.

But bold Roger Redbeard raced on, with dreams of gold to keep out the cold.

At last he got to the high back wall of the *Crooked Cow* pub.

Chapter 6
Hello Ello

Minnie the cat fell off his shoulder as Roger tried to scramble up the high brick wall. Ellie came after him. "Let me help you, Captain!" she said.

She cupped her hands, Roger put one foot in them and she lifted him up ... a little too fast. Roger shot over the wall like a cannonball and landed in the yard on his head.

He shook himself. He could hear faint sounds of laughter spilling out from the old bar. A tomcat howled close by. Minnie, the ship's parrot, howled back.

But closer still, someone moved in the shadows by the gate. "Who's that?" the bold pirate Captain hissed.

"Who's that?" said a shaky voice.

"Who's that, saying, 'Who's that?'"

"Who's that, saying, 'Who's that, saying, who's that?'" the shaky voice shook.

"I asked first," Roger Redbeard said. "Who are you?"

"Not telling," came the voice, and there was a soft, "*Sn-sn-sn-iff!*"

"Sniffle?" Roger said. "How did you get in here?"

"By the gate," the Cabin Boy replied. "It's open, you know."

Roger gave a sigh. A pirate's life is not an easy one. "Let Ellie in," he ordered. Then he began digging away at the hard earth in the corner. "You two find your own patch and let me know if you find anything."

After half an hour Roger was up to his neck in the hole. He'd hit solid rock. He looked out. He felt stiff. The yard was silent. "Ellie?"

"Aye aye, Captain?"

"Found anything?"

"Twenty-three worms and six dog bones."

"Sniffle?"

"*Sn-sn-sn-iff?*"

"Found anything?"

"Nah. Just an old brown case."

"A brown case!" the Captain cried. "What's in it? Gold, silver and jewels?"

"No-o. Nothing like that. It's full of bits of paper. Looks like five pound notes!"

"Treasure!" Ellie and the Captain cried at once. They slammed the case shut, snatched it up and rushed out into the lane. They also rushed out into the arms of a policeman.

"Now, what have we got here?" P.C. Ello asked. He took the case from the Captain's hands. "Had a report of noises in the back yard of the pub. Landlord was worried! I came round to see what was going on. You kids should be in bed at this time of night anyway."

The policeman pressed the catch of the old case and the lid sprang open. Piles of five pound notes fell out. The old policeman looked amazed. "And where did you get all this money from?"

"The back yard of the *Crooked Cow* pub," Ellie said sadly. "Roger worked out that it would be there."

"Did he now?" the policeman grinned. "Well, he's more clever than all the town's police! We've been looking for Baby-face Ging's loot for 25 years and have never found it."

"This is Ruby Rose's treasure hunt prize," Sniffle said.

Officer Ello smiled, "Nah! That's in the heart of the Town Chambers ... everyone knows that! All the golf club kids will end up there tomorrow. No, this is Baby-face

Ging's treasure all right. And you found it. You know what this means?"

Roger gave a sigh. He was worn out. It had been a bad day. "Bad news," was all he could say.

"Hah! No, me boy! More like a reward!" the policeman grinned. "I'll just look after these five pound notes for you ... they're *old* notes so they aren't worth anything. You call at the Town Chambers tomorrow after lunch and I'll bet the mayor will have a big reward for you."

The policeman stuffed the money back in the case, picked it up and plodded off down the back lane.

The pale street lamps glinted in Ellie's adoring eyes. "Oh, Roger," she said. "You are wonderful!"

Even in the dark, Roger's cheeks glowed
red.

"*Avast, me hearties!*" he roared. "We'll
meet tomorrow in the Town Chambers."

Chapter 7

Paper Pounds

Mayor Rupert Rose blinked and put on his glasses. "Now that the Council's work is done," he said, "I can present the prizes to the finders of the treasure!"

He took an envelope out of his pocket. "In this envelope there are two tickets to America ..."

"Oh, Roger," Ellie crooned. "You and I can go away together."

The pirate Captain looked a little unhappy. "Wouldn't you rather take Sniffle?" he asked.

Ellie punched him on the arm. "Would the winners of the treasure hunt please step up here," Mayor Rupert Rose went on.

Minnie wobbled on Captain Roger's shoulder as he stepped onto the floor of the Town Chambers with Ellie and Sniffle. The councillors gasped. The town clerk said something in the mayor's ear.

The mayor blinked again. "There seems to have been some mistake! These children found Baby-face Ging's treasure. They are not the winners of the treasure hunt!" he said.

"Ahhhh!" said all the councillors together.

The mayor looked under the table and pulled out the brown case the pirates had found. "Of course, the notes aren't worth anything now. You can have them all back. But we'd also like to give you a token of the town's thanks!" He pushed a chest at Roger and turned to the town clerk. "Now," he said with a smile, "where's my Ruby Rose and where are the real winners of the treasure hunt?"

The Pitt Street Pirates were led out of the Town Chambers in a hurry.

It was hot outside in the street. "Open the chest, Captain Roger," Sniffle said.

Roger opened it and looked inside. Ellie took something out of the chest.

"What is it? Gold? Silver? Holiday tickets to America?"

Roger shook his head. Ellie held up a roll of paper. She read out ...

The Town Council wishes to express its thanks to Roger Redwood and friends for finding the Ging Gang goodies.

Signed

Rupert Rose (Mayor)

"They didn't even get my name right," Roger said as they went sadly back to Pitt Street.

"Is that all?" Sniffle asked.

"There are one thousand useless old five pound notes. They aren't worth a penny!" said Roger, with a sigh.

"Will we build another *Titanic*?" Sniffle asked Roger as they walked past Mr Clark's shop.

Roger said nothing.

"Cheer up," Ellie said. "It could be worse."

The boy looked at her. "How? I'm a pirate who never stole anything. The treasure I found is not worth a penny. I'm a loser. How could it be worse?"

"You could be Ruby Rose!" Ellie grinned.

A cycle with gold and silver trim came round the corner on just two of its three wheels. Ruby Rose was peddling like mad.

"Help! Oh! Help!" she cried. "They want to kill me!"

"What's the matter, Ruby?" Ellie asked ... as if she didn't know.

"The golf club kids have worked all day to follow up the clues. They went mad when they had to wade across the Pitt Street Park lake in their best clothes," Ruby gasped and looked behind her in panic.

"It was worth it to get the treasure," said Roger.

"Yes! But when they got across the lake they found the clue had gone! And they blame me!" Ruby wailed.

"How did they know where the treasure was if they never found the clue?" asked Ellie.

"PC Ello told them. But they're still mad at me," Ruby replied.

"She's here!" a voice called out. A group of wet, muddy, angry rich kids came rushing round the corner and started to yell at Ruby Rose.

"Wahhhh!" she sobbed. "They say they're going to throw me in the lake!"

"You'll float," the Captain smiled. It was the first time he'd smiled for an hour.

"I won't float with this bike round my neck!" she shouted as she pedalled on as fast as she could.

The angry golf club kids vanished round the corner after Ruby. Roger Redbeard was rolling about on the ground, laughing. Even Sniffle saw the joke.

Ellie held up a grubby slip of paper with the last clue on it. "I think this is what got lost!" She too was laughing. "Hey, Captain! Who said we couldn't rob the rich?"

"Robbing is wrong!" a shaky old voice said from inside the shop. They were standing by the dusty windows of Mr Clark's shop and it was the old shopkeeper who had spoken.

The old man came to the door. "What have you got there, then?" he asked.

Roger showed him what was in the brown case. "Old five pound notes," he said, with a sigh. "Not worth a penny!"

Mr Clark looked in the box and shook his head. "Don't be stupid, lad! People collect old banknotes like those! They may not be worth five pounds each but they are worth something!"

"How much?" Sniffle asked.

"A pound at least!" the old man said. "I'll give you that!"

Roger looked at Ellie and she nodded. "A pound's better than nothing," she said.

The old man took the case and went back into the gloomy shop. He came out five minutes later with a fat bundle of money. "Here you are – there were one thousand notes in there – so here's one thousand pounds for you!"

Roger could hardly speak. "I thought you said one pound!"

"One pound for each note – one thousand notes, one thousand pounds!" the old man said, and smiled as he went slowly back into the shop. The three pirates went on down Pitt Street in a dream.

It was sunset before they woke up in the real world.

Roger sat on the warm doorstep and closed his eyes. The houses in the street turned into great galleons in his mind. "We'll build that new galleon. We'll sail the seven seas and bring back Spanish gold!"

"What will you spend your share of the treasure on?" Ellie asked Sniffle.

"A bike," Sniffle said. "And you?"

"A new collar for Minnie," she said, stroking the pirate cat till it purred loudly. "Then there are one or two videos I want to watch," Ellie said, looking at Roger.

"Pirate films?"

Ellie shook her head. "Romantic films," she said shyly. "Would you like to come and watch them with me, Roger?" She nudged him with her elbow.

Roger was looking across the street and seeing the great galleons in his mind. "I'll buy a new ship – a real sailing ship. It'll be the best on the seven seas."

"What'll you call it?" asked Ellie. "The *Fair Ellie?*"

Roger shook his head. "No-o," he said. "The first ship led us to the treasure. It was a lucky ship for us. Yes. I'll call my new ship *Titanic Two* ... I can't help thinking that's a *lucky* name for a ship!"

Who is Barrington Stoke?

Barrington Stoke went from place to place with his lamp in his hand. Everywhere he went, he told stories to children. Some were happy, some were sad, some were funny and some were scary.

The children always wanted more. When it got dark, they had to go home to bed. They went to look for Barrington Stoke the next day, but he had gone.

The children never forgot the stories. They told them to each other and to their children and their grandchildren. You see, good stories are magic and they can live for ever.

If you loved this story, why don't you read ...

The Hat Trick

by Terry Deary

Is there something you'll remember for as long as you'll live? When Seaburn football team meet their rivals, Jud has to step in as goalie. Can Jud save the day?

4u2read.ok!